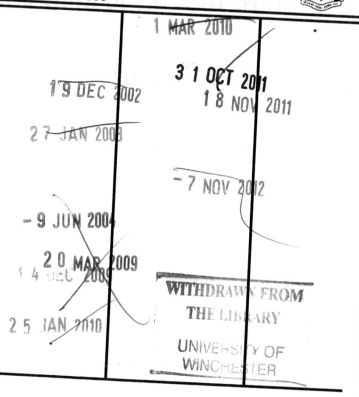

Pearson Education Limited
Edinburgh Gate, Harlow,
Essex CM20 2JE, England
and Associated Companies throughout the world.

ISBN 0 582 42738 X

This edition first published 2000

NEW EDITION

Copyright © Penguin Books Ltd 2000
Illustrations by Darren Dubicki
Cover design by Bender Richardson White

Typeset by Bender Richardson White
Set in 11/14pt Bembo
Printed and bound in Denmark by Norhaven A/S, Viborg

Published by Pearson Education Limited in association with
Penguin Books Ltd, both companies being subsidiaries of Pearson Plc

For a complete list of the titles available in the Penguin Readers series please write to your local
Pearson Education office or to: Marketing Department, Penguin Longman Publishing,
5 Bentinck Street, London W1M 5RN.

Contents

		page
Introduction		v
Chapter 1	Kelly Goes to London	1
Chapter 2	The Phone Call	4
Chapter 3	A Job is Hard to Find	8
Chapter 4	Max's Secret	14
Chapter 5	The Accident	19
Chapter 6	The Tall Man	24
Chapter 7	Escape!	30
Chapter 8	The Photo of the Year	33
Activities		39

Introduction

A 17-year-old girl was shot and killed yesterday during a six million pound bank robbery in London. A small, silver card was found next to the body. On it were just two letters – TM. Police are now looking for the famous 'Tall Man'. They describe him as 'Europe's most dangerous criminal'.

Sixteen-year-old Kelly Logan reads this newspaper story on the train to London. She is travelling there from her home in Scotland to stay with her Uncle Max. She plans to look for a job. But work is hard to find. Also, strange things start happening. Who is the mysterious person who phones her uncle's house? What is a man doing to Uncle Max's car? Max is a photographer, but he is being very secretive. Does he know more about the Tall Man than the police?

Stephen Rabley grew up in Devon, in the UK, and studied at Durham University. He taught English in Paris before he started writing books for English language students.

That was in 1979, and since then he has written many readers. Seven of them are Penguin Readers Easystarts.

Stephen Rabley now lives in London.

Chapter 1 Kelly Goes To London

Girl dies in bank robbery!
A 17-year-old girl was shot and killed yesterday during a six million pound bank robbery in London. A small, silver card was found next to the body. On it were just two letters – TM. Police are now looking for the famous 'Tall Man'. They describe him as 'Europe's most dangerous criminal'.

'He's also very clever,' said a crime expert last night. 'We don't really know what he looks like. There are no photographs of him. We only know that he's between forty-five and fifty. And he's over two metres tall.'

Kelly Logan put down her newspaper and looked out of the train window. 'How can people do things like that?' she thought. Then she remembered her grandfather's words at the station in Edinburgh: 'Listen, my girl. You've always lived on a small Scottish island. You don't understand what London is really like. I know you have to go there to find work. But please be careful.'

Kelly began to feel lonely and afraid. 'Perhaps I'm making a big mistake,' she thought. 'I'm only sixteen, I've never worked before and I failed all my exams at school. Who's going to give me a job?' Then she saw her face in the train window and began to smile. 'Stop feeling sad,' she told herself. 'Everything will be OK.' She looked at her watch. Six more hours to London.

A few minutes later, the train stopped at a station.

Suddenly, the door next to Kelly opened and a man walked in. He was about fifty, with a short beard and kind blue eyes. He smiled at Kelly, then sat down and began to read a book. Kelly could see the title out of the corner of her eye – *Murder in the Library.* The man saw Kelly's face and smiled. 'I love detective stories,' he said.

1

'Me too,' agreed Kelly. 'But I haven't read that one. Is it good?'

'Oh yes, very good,' the man answered. 'I've read it twice before. I don't know why I'm reading it again. I know how it ends!'

Just then, the train started. For a few minutes, Kelly and the man didn't speak. She looked out of the window and he read his book. Then he finished the last page.

'Who did it?' Kelly asked.

'The gardener,' the man answered. 'He did it last time, too!' They both laughed, then the man asked, 'Are you going to London?'

'Yes. I've never been there before.'

The man looked surprised. 'What an adventure for you!' he said with a bright smile. 'Are you on holiday?'

'No,' Kelly said. 'I'm going there to look for a job.' Suddenly, she began to feel sad again. 'Would you like an apple?' she said quickly. 'I've got lots in my suitcase.'

The man smiled. 'Yes, why not?' he said. As Kelly opened her suitcase, he looked at her. How old was she? Sixteen? Seventeen? She was more like a boy than a girl, really, with her very short brown hair and green eyes. Even her clothes were like boys' clothes. She was wearing tennis shoes, jeans and a short black jacket. 'Where are your parents?' he asked.

Kelly passed him an apple. 'They died in a plane crash when I was very young,' she said. 'But you don't want to hear all about me, Mr . . .'

'Harris, my name's Felix Harris,' the man said. 'And I do want to hear. I'm a doctor and doctors are very good at listening. Now, you were saying . . .'

'Well, if you're sure?' Kelly said.

For the next twenty minutes she told Dr Harris about herself. She talked about her life on the Isle of Skye with her grandfather . . . She told him about failing all her exams . . . everything. 'Then last month my dad's brother, Uncle Max, sent a letter,' she said. 'He's a newspaper photographer. He's got a big house in a part of north London called Highgate. Do you know it?'

'Yes,' said Dr Harris.

'Well, he lives there with his son, Adam. Adam's a student at London University. He's studying French, I think. In the letter, Uncle Max said, "Come and live with me and Adam for a few months. Then you can look for a job in London." '

'Right. And what kind of job do you want to do?' the doctor asked.

'Anything!' Kelly answered. Then, with a quick laugh, she added, 'Well, I *really* want to be a mechanic. I'm not very clever, but I'm good at repairing things.'

Dr Harris looked at her. 'I think you'll be OK,' he said. 'I can see it in your eyes. Some people are losers and others are winners. You're a winner.'

Five hours later, the train arrived at King's Cross station in

London. 'Well, here we are,' Doctor Harris said. 'Is anyone meeting you?'

'Yes,' Kelly said. 'Uncle Max is working in France for a few days, but Adam's meeting me.'

The doctor smiled. 'Good luck, Kelly,' he said. 'I hope you find a job. And I hope you like London. It's really a very nice place.' He pointed to her newspaper. 'You mustn't believe everything that you read about it.'

'Goodbye, Dr Harris,' Kelly said. 'And thanks for listening. It really helped.'

A minute later, Kelly was standing on the platform with her suitcase. Now she was only one of thousands of people at King's Cross station. For a minute she didn't know what to do. Then suddenly, she saw a young man coming towards her through the crowd. He was thin, about nineteen or twenty, with small, round glasses and long red hair. Was it Adam? Kelly wasn't sure. Quickly, she took a photo of Adam from her pocket. Yes, that was him. He wasn't wearing glasses in the photo, but the intelligent, friendly face was the same.

'OK, Kelly,' she said to herself. 'This is where your new life starts.' She picked up her suitcase and walked towards the face.

Chapter 2   The Phone Call

Outside King's Cross station, Adam Logan put Kelly's suitcase in the back of a very old car. He was wearing jeans and a T-shirt with the word *JAZZ* on the front. Suddenly, he noticed Kelly's face. She was standing next to the car with her mouth half-open, looking around her at the taxis, buses and cars.

'Welcome to London, cousin!' Adam said. 'I'm afraid it's a bit noisier here than on the Isle of Skye.'

Kelly put both hands into the pockets of her jacket and smiled.

'Before we go to Highgate, I'll give you a tour of the city,' Adam offered. 'Or are you too tired?'

'No, I'm not tired,' Kelly replied. She smiled again and opened the car door. 'Let's go.'

For the next hour, Adam drove Kelly around the centre of London. He showed her all the famous places: Buckingham Palace, Trafalgar Square, the Houses of Parliament, Oxford Street. As they drove around Hyde Park Corner, she said nervously, 'Everyone drives so fast here.'

Adam smiled. 'You won't notice it after a few weeks,' he said.

Kelly looked out of the car window. She began to think of the

empty bedroom in her grandfather's small, stone house. Then she thought of her friends on the island, and . . .

'Do you see that bank?' Adam asked suddenly. He pointed to a building as they drove past it. 'There was a big robbery there yesterday.'

Kelly looked. Three policemen were standing in front of the building. Suddenly, she remembered the newspaper story about the Tall Man and the small silver card which was found next to the body. She remembered the two letters on it − *TM*.

'Yes, I read about it,' she said.

Twenty minutes later, they arrived in Highgate. It was a quieter part of the city, with narrow, pretty streets, small shops and lots of trees. Adam stopped the car in front of a large, old house on the top of a hill.

'Well, here we are,' he said. '45 Cranley Road − the home of Max Logan, Adam Logan, and now, Kelly Logan.' At the front door, Adam took a key out of his pocket. 'The car belongs to Dad, not me,' he said. 'That's mine.' He pointed to a motorbike across the street.

'Oh, great, I love motorbikes!' Kelly said. 'Lots of my friends on Skye have them. It's a '94 Suzuki 750, isn't it?'

Adam looked at her. He opened his mouth to speak. Then he closed it again. Finally, he said, 'That's right,' and he put the key in the door.

Kelly liked her uncle's house immediately. It was warm and friendly with lots of books, paintings and photographs everywhere. Adam went into the kitchen. 'Coffee?' he shouted.

'Yes please,' answered Kelly from the living-room. 'Black and no sugar.'

After a minute, Adam returned with two cups. 'Here's your coffee,' he said.

'Oh thanks.' Kelly took one of the cups and sat down on a soft green chair. 'How long will Uncle Max be in France?' she asked.

'Two more days,' Adam said. 'Or is it three? I'm not sure.' He laughed. 'I don't see him very often. He's always working and I'm usually at college or with friends.'

'Of course,' said Kelly.

Adam put his glasses on and looked at her. Then he said, 'You're very brave, you know.'

Kelly smiled. 'Brave? What do you mean?'

'Well,' Adam continued, 'you're only sixteen. You've never been to London before. You don't really know Dad or me. But here you are – starting a completely new life. I think that's brave.'

'Not really,' said Kelly. 'I couldn't stay on Skye after I left school. There are no jobs there for young people. So, when Uncle Max wrote . . .'

Suddenly, the phone rang.

'Excuse me,' Adam said, and went to answer it. When he came back, he said, 'That was Phil – a friend. He's going to a party and he wants me to go, too.' He stopped. 'Is that OK? I mean, you're welcome to . . .'

'No thanks,' Kelly said. 'I'm really tired. I just want to have a bath and go to bed.'

'Are you sure?'

'Yes, I'm sure. Have a good time and I'll see you tomorrow. Oh, and Adam – thanks for the tour.'

Alone in the house, Kelly went upstairs and found her room.

Half an hour later, she was drying her hair after a bath when the phone rang again. She ran downstairs and answered it. 'Hello?' There was no answer, but somebody was listening – Kelly was sure of it. 'Who's there?'

Again, no answer. Then a man's voice said, very quickly and quietly, 'Where's Logan? I want to speak to Max Logan.'

'I'm sorry, he's not here,' said Kelly. 'He's abroad for a few days. Can I take a message?'

'Tell him that Drake phoned – Gordon Drake. And tell him

the visitor is arriving in December. That's all.'

'Wait!' said Kelly. 'I don't understand. Who's the . . .'

But it was too late. Kelly put down the phone and looked at it. 'That was strange,' she thought. 'He sounded almost . . . afraid.'

She went back upstairs. Between the bathroom and her own room, Kelly passed a half-open door. She could see a large desk with a computer on it. There were two cameras on the desk, too. 'That's Uncle Max's office,' she thought.

A big black book was in the corner of the room. On its cover was the word *Photos*. Slowly, Kelly put one hand against the door and opened it a little more. 'No. I mustn't,' she told herself. Then she thought, 'Well, maybe I'll just have a quick look.'

She went into the room and sat at the desk. She opened the big black book. Inside were newspaper photographs, her uncle's photographs. There were pictures of politicians, pop singers and sports stars – all kinds of famous people. Finally, Kelly turned to the last page of the book. It was empty except for three words in large writing at the top of the page: *THE TALL MAN*.

Chapter 3   A Job is Hard to Find

The next day, Kelly woke up very late. She looked at her watch – it was 10.30 – then sat up in bed. 'All right, Kelly Logan,' she thought. 'Today, you must start looking for a job.' She dressed quickly and went downstairs. Adam was in the kitchen, drinking coffee. There was a bag on the table next to him.

'Good morning,' said Kelly.

'Hi,' Adam replied with a tired smile.

'How was the party?'

'Great,' Adam said, 'but I got home at three o'clock. That wasn't so great.' He poured her a cup of coffee.

'Thanks,' Kelly said.

Suddenly, Adam looked at his watch. 'Is that the time? I must go!' He put a book in his bag and got up. 'Listen,' he said, 'I'll be home this evening at about six. Will you be OK?'

Kelly laughed. 'Yes, of course I will. I'm going to start looking for a job today.'

Adam took a key out of his bag and put it on the table.

'That's for the front door,' he said. Then he took a newspaper out of his bag. 'And you'll need this. It's yesterday evening's newspaper. You'll find lots of job advertisements in there.'

'Thanks,' Kelly said.

Adam smiled and picked up his bag. 'See you later, OK?'

Kelly read all the job advertisements carefully. Two of them looked really interesting. The first was for a young person 'to work in the busy office of a record company'. The second said, 'London Sports is looking for a friendly young person to work in its Oxford Street shop.' Kelly put circles around both advertisements with a red pen. Then she took the newspaper to the phone.

Five minutes later, she was back in the kitchen again. The record company wanted somebody who was over eighteen. The job at the sports shop was already taken. 'This isn't going to be easy,' Kelly thought. She looked at the front page of the newspaper: 'Britain's Biggest Robbery,' it said. Then she turned to the job advertisements and began to read them again.

♦

Two days later, Max Logan returned from France. Kelly wasn't there when he arrived. She was at her first job interview. But when she opened the front door of 45 Cranley Road at five o'clock, she saw a big green bag and two metal camera cases.

'Is that you, Kelly?' said a deep voice from the kitchen. The door to the kitchen opened. There was Max Logan, wearing jeans and an old blue jacket. He had a pipe in his mouth.

'Hello, Uncle Max,' Kelly said with a happy smile. 'Welcome home.'

Max made tea and told Kelly about his visit to Paris. Then he said, 'Now I want to hear all about you. Do you think you're going to like London?'

'I want to,' Kelly said, 'but it's so different. On Skye, everything's clean and green and quiet. Here, everything's . . .'

'Dirty, grey and noisy? You're right,' Max said. He smiled. 'What about a job? Have you found one yet?'

Kelly looked down. 'No, not yet. But I went to an interview at a pizza restaurant this afternoon.' Max looked surprised. 'I know, I know. It's not a very good job,' Kelly said, 'but I've spoken to lots of other companies. They all want people who've passed exams. What can I do? I've got to start somewhere.'

'Of course,' Max agreed. 'When will you know about the job in the restaurant?'

'They asked me to phone tomorrow morning,' Kelly said.

'Good,' Max replied. He took Kelly's hands. 'I want you to know something,' he said. 'You can stay here for as long as you like. Agreed?'

Kelly smiled. 'Thanks,' she said. 'You're the best uncle in the world.' They talked about Kelly's grandfather and Adam for a few minutes. Then Kelly said, 'I nearly forgot. A man phoned last Friday and left a message. His name was Gordon Drake. He said, "The visitor is arriving in December."'

Max slowly turned the cup that he was holding in his hands. 'Is that all?'

'Yes. What did he mean?' Kelly asked.

'Oh, it's not important,' Max replied. 'Now – more tea?'

◆

The next morning, there was some bad news for Kelly from the pizza restaurant. 'I'm sorry,' said the manager, when Kelly phoned.

'We liked you, but . . . well, you've never worked in a restaurant before, and . . .'

'I know,' said Kelly, 'but I learn very quickly. Can't you . . . ?'

'I'm sorry,' said the manager again, then he put the phone down.

'I'm never going to get a job,' Kelly thought.

Adam came out of the living-room. He looked at Kelly. 'I heard,' he said. 'Listen, Dad and I are going to the cinema tonight. Do you want to come?'

'Thanks, but I'm trying to save my money,' Kelly said.

'That's OK,' Adam replied. 'We'll pay for you.'

'No, it's *not* OK!' Kelly said angrily. 'You and Uncle Max can't pay for everything.' She stopped and looked down at the floor. 'I've got to have a job and my own money,' she said more quietly. 'You can understand that, can't you?'

◆

Kelly went to eight interviews in the next two weeks, but at the end of each one the answer was always 'no'. Her ninth was at a hotel in Mayfair, one of the richest parts of London. The advertisement said: 'We're looking for a young person who wants to learn. Must like hard work. If this describes you, write to: John Miller, Manager, The Imperial Hotel, Mayfair.'

At the interview, John Miller was very friendly. He gave Kelly some coffee, then asked her a lot of questions. 'Well, that's all fine,' he said after ten minutes.

'Really?' Kelly asked.

'Yes,' John Miller replied. He smiled. 'OK, you haven't worked before, and you haven't passed any exams, but you're intelligent and friendly. You really want to learn and work hard. I can see that. Oh yes, I think we . . .' Suddenly, he stopped. 'Aaaahh,' he said slowly, looking at Kelly's letter.

'What is it?' she asked.

John Miller wasn't smiling now. 'I'm afraid I didn't notice your age. You're only sixteen. I'm sorry, but that's too young. We want somebody who's over eighteen. My secretary didn't put that in the advertisement.'

'But . . .' Kelly began.

John Miller stood up. 'I'm so sorry,' he repeated, opening the door.

On the bus back to Highgate, Kelly sat upstairs and looked out of the window. It was raining. At Highgate, she got off and started to walk up the hill to Max's house. 'I can't continue with this,' she thought. 'London was a good idea, but it hasn't worked and I must accept that. Enough is enough. I must go back to Scotland. I'll tell Max and Adam tonight.'

Kelly was nearly at the house when she saw Adam. He was on his motorbike. He stopped in front of the house and got off quickly. Then he ran to meet her. 'Well, did you get the job?' he asked.

'No,' Kelly answered sadly. 'I'm too young.'

Adam took off his crash helmet. 'Good,' he said.

'What do you mean?' asked Kelly. 'What's good about it?'

Adam smiled. 'Well, who wants to work in a hotel when you can work in a motorbike garage?'

Kelly looked at her cousin. 'Adam, what are you talking about?' she asked.

'I went to see some friends today – George and Rosa Carter. Dad and I have known them for years. They've got a motorbike garage near here – in Kentish Town.'

'And?'

'And they need some help for the next few months. There's a girl, Jan, who usually helps George with the paperwork. But she's going to have a baby.'

'So *you* said . . . ?'

Adam smiled. 'They want to see you tomorrow morning – ten o'clock.'

Kelly threw her arms around her cousin. 'That's wonderful. Oh Adam – thanks. Let's tell Uncle Max.'

They ran into the house and Kelly took off her wet coat. 'Uncle Max,' she called, 'I've got some good . . .'

Then she saw that her uncle was talking on the phone. Quickly, he looked at Kelly and put a finger to his mouth.

'Sorry,' Kelly said.

'Listen, Drake,' Max said. 'I must know where the December meeting is going to be. Yes, of course it's dangerous, I understand that. OK, OK. Do that and call me again soon.' Max put down the phone, walked upstairs to his office and closed the door.

'What was that about?' Adam asked Kelly. Then he saw her face. 'Are you OK?' he asked. 'You look . . . strange . . .'

'What? Oh, it's nothing,' she said. 'I'm cold, that's all. Tell me more about George and Rosa's garage.'

Chapter 4   Max's Secret

The next morning, Kelly arrived early at the Carters' garage. There were some motorbikes parked outside a large pair of metal doors. A sign on the door said *R and G Garage*. Kelly knocked and waited.

After a few seconds, a woman in a pair of very dirty dungarees opened one of the doors. She was small, with short dark hair and clear brown skin.

'Ah, you're Kelly,' she said with a big smile. 'Come in. I'm Rosa. It's nice to meet you.' Then she turned around and shouted, 'George! Adam Logan's cousin is here.'

Inside the garage, there were more motorbikes than outside. Somewhere a radio was playing loud pop music. Behind one of the motorbikes, Kelly noticed a man. Suddenly, the music stopped and he stood up. He had long black hair, a beard and a big gold ring in his left ear. His dungarees were even dirtier than Rosa's.

'Oh yes – hello Kelly,' he said. 'Adam told us about you. Let's all go into the office. It's quieter in there.'

The 'office' was a small room full of pieces of paper and bits of motorbikes. George cleared some books off a chair and said, 'Please, Kelly, sit down.' Then he and Rosa told her about the job. They wanted somebody to help with the paperwork and the repair work at the garage for three months.

'And only three months. I hope you understand that,' Rosa said. Next, she and George asked Kelly lots of questions about herself.

After a few minutes, George looked down at his hands. 'Well Kelly, we're really looking for somebody a bit older – somebody who's worked in a garage before.'

'I know I'm only sixteen,' said Kelly quickly, 'but I've always been interested in motorbikes – always! On Skye I repaired all my friends' motorbikes.'

'Do you know how to ride one?' Rosa asked.

Kelly looked at the floor. 'No, I'm too young for that,' she said. The room became very quiet. 'Listen,' Kelly said, 'I don't mind that it's only for a few months. It's a beginning. That's what I need. I'll work really hard – I promise. I know I can do it. Just try me. Please.'

George looked at Rosa, then Rosa opened the office door. 'Will you wait outside for five minutes, Kelly?'

They were the longest five minutes of Kelly's life, but finally the door opened again.

'You can come in now,' Rosa said.

In the office, Kelly didn't sit down.

'We've talked about it carefully,' George said. 'And these are the facts. You're very young, you don't know London, and you've never worked in a garage before.'

Kelly closed her eyes. 'It's going to happen again,' she thought.

Then she heard George say, 'But . . . we both like you. And it's clear that you want to work hard.' He laughed. 'So, you start tomorrow. Agreed?'

Kelly opened her eyes again. 'Do you mean it?' she asked.

'We mean it,' Rosa replied, laughing. 'Welcome to the R and G Garage, Kelly.'

That evening, Kelly phoned her grandfather and told him the good news. Then Max and Adam took her out to a French restaurant.

'Well, you've done it – you've got a job,' Adam said after the meal. 'Dad and I are both really pleased.'

Kelly smiled. 'Thanks,' she said. 'Thanks for everything.'

♦

The next two months were the busiest of Kelly's life. She worked with Rosa in the R and G's office every morning, and repaired motorbikes with George each afternoon.

One day, George pointed at her and laughed. 'Look at you!' he said. 'You've only been here a few weeks and your dungarees are dirtier than mine!'

Kelly looked at herself, then she laughed, too. He was right.

Slowly, Kelly was beginning to enjoy her new life in London. She was always busy during the day, and she started to go out more often in the evenings. Sometimes at weekends she went to the cinema with Adam and his university friends.

One Tuesday evening, she and her uncle were watching television together. On the news, there was a story about a crime in France.

'Thieves shot and killed a rich businessman in his house outside Paris earlier today,' the newsreader said. 'Then they stole three paintings by Matisse. After the robbery, a small silver card was found next to the dead businessman. On it were two letters – *TM*.'

Kelly looked at her uncle. He was listening carefully to every word. The newsreader had another man with him, a crime expert.

'What do we know about the Tall Man?' the newsreader asked.

'Not very much, I'm afraid. But we do know that he's very, *very* dangerous. This man will kill if he has to. He's already killed three people.'

'Do we have any idea what he looks like? I understand that the police have no photographs of him.'

'Yes, that's right,' the expert said. 'We know that he's between forty-five and fifty and over two metres tall. But that's all. There are no photos of him anywhere.'

Max smiled as the expert said these words. Then the phone rang. Max got up to answer it. He closed the door behind him and spoke in a very quiet voice. But Kelly could still hear what he was saying.

'Yes, I was just watching it,' he said. Then, a few seconds later, 'I've told you before. The Tall Man is coming to Britain soon. I know when. I know where, too, but I can't tell you any more than that. You'll just have to believe me.' There was a short silence. Then Kelly heard her uncle say, 'It'll be the photograph of the year. I'm going to get it and it'll be in your newspaper.'

◆

The next morning, Kelly came downstairs to breakfast as usual. Her uncle was already reading the morning newspaper and didn't notice her. She was just pouring herself a cup of tea when he said, 'No, it's not *possible*!'

Kelly looked at him. 'What is it?' she asked.

'Nothing,' her uncle replied. He put the paper down and looked out of the window. Kelly looked at the newspaper.

A man's body was found in the River Thames yesterday evening. There was a knife in his back. He was later named as Gordon Drake. Police believe that Drake knew many of London's top criminals. They think that one of these men . . .

Kelly stopped reading. Her eyes went back to the name of the man. 'Drake. Wasn't that the man who I spoke to on the phone? Don't you remember? That first evening?'

'Please, Kelly. Don't ask me any questions,' Max said.

'But he's dead! Murdered!' Kelly shouted. 'Was he trying to help you? Did he know something about . . . ?' She wanted to say 'the Tall Man', but she stopped.

'I can't talk about this to anybody, Kelly,' her uncle said, and got up from the table. Kelly watched him.

'Is your life in danger, too?' she asked. 'Is it?'

Her uncle didn't answer.

Chapter 5   The Accident

A few days later, Kelly got home a little earlier than usual. It was a cold December evening and snow was falling softly. As she walked up Cranley Road, she thought about her job. She was enjoying it more and more every day, but she remembered Rosa's words: 'It's only for three months. I hope you understand that.' And after those three months?

Suddenly, she saw a dark shape near the top of the hill. It was a man in a long black coat, standing next to Max's car. He was putting something into a bag.

'That's not Uncle Max,' she thought. The man picked up his bag and walked away. Kelly heard the sound of a motorbike behind her. It was Adam. He waved and stopped.

'Hi! Do you want to go to a jazz club tonight?' he shouted.

'What?' Kelly asked quietly. She was still watching the dark shape of the man.

'Do you want to go to a jazz club? I'm going with two friends.'

As the man turned a corner, Kelly saw his face for a second. His skin was very pale, and he had short dark hair and a moustache.

'Well?' Adam asked. There was no answer. 'Kelly! Wake up!' he said, laughing.

Kelly turned and looked at him. 'Sorry,' she said. 'I was just . . . oh well, it doesn't matter.'

Adam closed his eyes and spoke very slowly. 'Do you, or do you not, want to go to a jazz club tonight?'

'Well, I'd like to,' Kelly said, 'but I've got to write some letters, and . . .'

'You can write them tomorrow. And if you say, "No, I can't" . . .' He picked up some snow, made a ball and lifted the ball above his head.

Kelly started to laugh and put both hands in front of her face. 'All right. All right! I'll come.'

◆

They had a very good time at the club. Kelly danced and forgot about the man in the black coat. It was late when they got home. As Adam parked his motorbike, Kelly noticed something strange. The car was gone.

'Do you know where your dad is?' she asked.

'No,' Adam replied. 'He was in his office when we left.'

Inside the house, Adam made some tea. Kelly went into the living-room to put on some music. She passed the telephone answering–machine. A small red light showed that there were two messages. 'Perhaps Grandad called,' she thought, and pressed *PLAY*. She was right – the first message *was* from her grandfather. It was very short: 'Kelly, this is Grandad. I hate these machines, so I'll call again tomorrow, OK? Lots of love.' Kelly smiled, but then the second message began and the smile left her face.

'This is the Whittington Hospital. Mr Max Logan was brought here at ten o'clock this evening after a car accident. Please call us as soon as possible.'

◆

Fifteen minutes later, Kelly and Adam arrived at the hospital. At the desk, Adam said, 'I'm Max Logan's son. Can you tell me where he is, please?'

'Sit down and I'll find out for you,' said the woman behind the desk. It was 1.30 a.m.

After a few minutes, a doctor arrived. He was about fifty, with a short beard and kind blue eyes. 'Hello,' he said. 'You're Mr Logan's son. Then he saw Kelly. 'Well, what a surprise!' he said.

Suddenly, Kelly remembered. He was the man on the train. 'Dr Harris!' she said. 'I don't believe it!'

Two minutes later, Adam and Kelly were sitting in Dr Harris's office. 'I'm afraid the news isn't good,' he said. 'He's broken both legs and his right arm.'

Adam's face was white. 'How did the accident happen? Do you know?' he asked.

'No, not really,' Dr Harris said. 'The police found his car at the bottom of Highgate Hill. They think the brakes stopped working.'

'Can we see him?' asked Kelly.

'Yes, but only for a minute. We've given him something. He'll be asleep soon.'

Max's room was in another part of the hospital. Dr Harris took Adam and Kelly there. Before he opened the door, he said, 'Remember – just a minute.'

Inside the room, Max was lying completely flat with his eyes closed.

'Dad? Dad, can you hear me?' asked Adam. Max's eyes opened slowly. 'Don't try to speak, Dad. Just listen. Everything's going to be OK. Do you understand?'

Max began to open and close his mouth. At first he made no sound, then a few words came out, 'The c-, in the car . . . a note. He's coming . . . he's coming, he's . . .' Then Max closed his eyes and stopped speaking.

'He's fallen asleep,' said Dr Harris. 'Why don't you go home and do the same? Come again tomorrow.'

Outside the hospital it was still snowing. Adam started the motorbike, but Kelly put a hand on his shoulder. 'Wait a minute!' she said. 'I've had an idea.'

Ten minutes later, they stopped outside Highgate police station.

'I don't understand,' Adam said. 'Why did you want to come here?'

Kelly got off the motorbike. 'I'll tell you in a few minutes,' she said. 'Just wait here, OK?' Then she ran up the steps into the police station.

At three o'clock exactly, Kelly came out again. She was carrying a metal camera case.

'Well?' Adam said.

'I was right. They brought the car here after the accident.'

'So?'

'So I said, "My uncle needs his camera case."'

'But he doesn't.'

'Adam, I know that,' Kelly said. 'I really wanted to look at the brakes on the car. They didn't stop working. They were cut.'

'Cut!'

Kelly told Adam about the man she saw outside 45 Cranley Road.

'But I still don't understand,' Adam said. 'Are you telling me that this man tried to *kill* Dad?'

'I think so,' Kelly said. 'And look at this. I found it in the car under the front seat. The police didn't see me take it.' She took a piece of paper out of her pocket. On it were the words: 'Tall Man will arrive on KALADIS, Harwich, 19th December 7 a.m. for December meeting.' Below that, in smaller letters, was '18642, Exit C.'

Adam read it and looked at his cousin. 'Is this what Dad was talking about at the hospital – a note?'

'I think so,' Kelly replied. 'And do you remember that he said, "he's coming"? I think he meant the Tall Man. Oh, Adam, don't you understand? Uncle Max was driving to Harwich to try to get a photo of the Tall Man. That's when his car crashed.'

Adam held up his hands. 'Wait a minute,' he said. 'I *don't* understand. Go back to the beginning.'

Kelly put down the heavy camera case. 'OK,' she said. First, she told Adam about the empty page in Max's book of photos. Next, she described the strange phone call from Gordon Drake on the same evening. Then there were the other calls. One was minutes after Adam told her about the R and G Garage. Another was after the news of the robbery in France. Finally, there was the man in the black coat earlier that evening. Adam listened to his cousin carefully. 'Uncle Max wanted to get a photo – the first photo ever – of the Tall Man,' Kelly continued. 'Gordon Drake was helping him. Then Drake was murdered. Now someone has tried to kill Uncle Max.'

'Well, we must tell the police,' said Adam, getting off the motorbike.

Kelly put a hand on his arm. 'No,' she replied. 'There isn't time. Think, Adam. The police will want more than a piece of paper. They'll want to talk to Max before they do anything. The Tall Man is arriving in four hours – there isn't time!'

Adam looked at the note again. 'You're right,' he said, 'but I still don't understand everything. What does "Kaladis" mean, and "December meeting" and "18642" and "Exit C"?'

'I don't know,' Kelly answered softly. 'I only know that we've got to go to Harwich – now! Uncle Max can't get a photo of the Tall Man, but we can. Please Adam – let's do it for your father.'

Adam looked at his cousin for a long time. Then he said, 'All right. We'll do it.' He put on his crash helmet. 'Ready?' he asked.

Kelly climbed on behind him. 'Ready,' she replied.

Chapter 6   The Tall Man

At 6.15, Adam and Kelly arrived in the small east-coast port. For ten minutes, they drove through the quiet, snow-covered streets. Then they saw the sign that they were looking for: *Port of Harwich – Ferry Arrivals*. They turned right and there, in front of them, was the long, low ferry building. They parked and went inside.

Kelly took off her crash helmet and looked around. It was early, but there were already lots of people there. 'We need a timetable,' she said. 'Look! There's the information desk. We can get one there.'

A minute later, she and Adam sat down on two plastic chairs. Kelly opened the timetable. 'Yes, here it is,' she said. 'There's only one ship arriving at seven o'clock. It's a ferry from Rotterdam, and its name is . . .'

Adam smiled. 'The *Kaladis*.' He looked at his watch. 'OK, we've got half an hour. First, let's get the camera ready. Then we'll go outside and wait.'

Twenty minutes later, they left the ferry building. Outside, it was still snowing. They walked along one side of the building. Then they turned a corner and both stopped.

'There it is,' Adam said quietly. The tall, dark shape of a ferry was moving slowly towards the dock. Kelly could see a name in white letters on the front of the ship – *Kaladis*. 'Now what do we do?' Adam asked.

Kelly looked along the side of the ferry. Suddenly, she saw a big metal door. There was a sign on it: *Exit A*. Kelly took the piece of paper from Max's car out of her pocket. She pointed at the door. 'Look. That's Exit A. We want Exit C. It's at the other end. Let's hurry.'

Together the two cousins ran quickly and quietly between the lorries and wooden boxes on the busy dock. They finally stopped behind one of the biggest boxes. The *Kaladis* was now in front of them. Kelly and Adam looked up. There it was – Exit C.

'Good,' Adam said. 'Nobody can see us here, but we can see everything.'

Two men slowly began to open the big metal door. Next they placed a short bridge between the ship and the dock. Quickly, Kelly opened the metal camera case. The first passengers were starting to get off the *Kaladis*.

'Well, this is it,' she said.

A long line of people walked down the small metal bridge and into the ferry building. One or two were quite tall, but none of them was two metres. Adam and Kelly watched each face carefully.

'Where is he?' Kelly asked quietly. Fifty or sixty passengers left the ship, then the line of people ended. Two minutes later, the Exit C door closed with a loud crash.

Kelly turned to Adam. 'Where is he? I don't understand.'

'Perhaps he didn't come,' Adam said in a tired voice.

Slowly, Kelly put the camera back into its metal case. She felt very angry.

'Now we'll never get a photo of the Tall Man,' she thought.

Suddenly, Adam pointed at the *Kaladis*. 'Wait a minute,' he said. 'Do you see those containers?'

Kelly looked at the ship. 'You mean those big metal boxes that they're lifting onto the lorries?'

'Yes,' Adam said. 'Give me the piece of paper that you found in Dad's car.' Kelly gave him the note and he read it quickly. Then he pointed at one of the containers and smiled. '18642,' he said quietly.

Kelly looked. He was right. There was a container with *18642* on its side on one of the lorries. 'Are you thinking what I'm thinking?' Kelly asked.

'Yes, I am,' Adam replied. 'Let's get the motorbike. We're going to follow that lorry.'

It was almost daylight as Kelly and Adam drove out of Harwich behind the lorry. There were three exit roads from the docks – Exit A, Exit B and Exit C. The lorry followed the signs for Exit C.

'Of course!' Adam said. 'That's what it meant.'

The lorry turned left. A few seconds later, Adam did the same. Now they were on the road to London. Kelly looked up at the sky. It was beginning to snow again.

After forty minutes, they were nearly in London. 'I think our friend's going to Limehouse,' Adam said. 'He's following all the signs to it.'

'Where's that?' Kelly shouted against the snow and wind.

'It's a part of east London, by the river,' Adam replied. 'There are lots of old buildings, canals and warehouses there.'

Adam was right. Ten minutes later, the lorry turned into a narrow street in Limehouse. A sign on the wall said *Mill Way*. At the end of the street, there was a warehouse with a lot of broken windows. In front of it there were two big metal doors. The lorry stopped in front of them.

After a few seconds, the doors opened and the lorry drove inside. Adam and Kelly got off the motorbike at the end of the street. Kelly hid behind a building on the corner, but continued watching. Adam was behind her.

'What can you see?' he asked in a low voice.

'There are some men standing in front of the warehouse doors. They're closing the doors now . . . One man has just locked them . . . The others have gone inside . . . but he's still standing in the street,' Kelly answered. She took off her crash helmet.

'I think I understand it all now,' she said. 'They put the Tall Man in a container in Rotterdam. He crosses to Harwich. They bring the container here and open it. Then he meets all the people who work for him here in Britain.'

'Yes,' Adam said quietly. 'The December meeting. It happens every year. Then he gets back in the container, they drive him back to Harwich, and he's in Rotterdam again by the next day. Simple! And very, very clever.'

'We've got to get into that warehouse,' Kelly said.

'Yes,' Adam replied. 'But not this way. Let's try the back of the building.'

They ran quickly and silently around the corner and down the street next to Mill Way. On each side of them there were tall, empty buildings with broken windows.

'That warehouse at the end,' said Adam. 'The one next to the river.'

'Yes,' agreed Kelly. She could see some metal stairs going up the side of the warehouse. 'Look – there's a fire-escape.'

Suddenly, a man in a long grey coat walked around the side of the warehouse. Kelly and Adam quickly hid behind a parked car. 'I don't think he saw us,' said Adam softly.

They waited for a few seconds, then Kelly slowly stood up.

'He's gone,' she said. 'Let's go.' They ran towards the fire-escape and began to climb it. On the first floor, Kelly looked to her right and saw a broken window. She pointed at it. Making as little noise as possible, Kelly climbed over the side of the fire-escape and through the window. Then Adam passed her the camera case and followed.

The cousins were in a small, empty room. It had dirty walls and a wooden floor. Kelly looked at Adam and put a finger to her mouth. She could hear voices. They were coming from below. Looking down, she noticed something. In one corner of the room there was an opening in the floor. She pointed at it and Adam smiled. Then, very slowly and quietly, they both lay down on the floor.

There, about ten metres below them, was the top of the container from the *Kaladis*. Standing around it were five men. Two men were talking quietly. One was putting some papers on a small white table. He had very pale skin, dark hair and a moustache. Kelly's eyes grew wide with surprise. He was the man in Cranley Road, next to Max's car. Three of the men, Adam noticed, were holding guns. Quietly, Kelly took the camera out of the metal case.

A few minutes later, the man at the table spoke. 'If everyone's ready, we can begin now.' All the others stopped talking. 'Let's meet our visitor,' the man said. 'Open the container, Terry.'

'OK, Mr Strang,' he said. With a key, he opened six large locks. Then he pulled hard and the end of the container slowly opened.

At first, Kelly and Adam couldn't see anything. The inside of the big metal box was completely dark. They waited. For ten long seconds nothing happened. Then suddenly, there was a shadow at the entrance of the container. It was a man of about fifty. He had silver hair and was wearing a dark suit. Kelly and Adam watched carefully.

Strang walked towards the container. 'Welcome, sir. Welcome!' he said. He held his right hand in front of him. Slowly, the man in the container stepped down onto the ground. He looked at the hand in front of him, but didn't touch it. The Tall Man's height became clear. Strang was shorter than his 'visitor' by almost half a metre.

Kelly looked through the camera. She could see the Tall Man's face clearly. He had cold, blue eyes. She moved a little to the left. Then, when she was ready, someone suddenly stood up in front of him.

'Sit down!' thought Kelly. The man talked and talked, but finally he sat down. Kelly looked through the camera again. 'That's better,' she thought. 'Now, don't move. Please . . . don't . . . move.' Quickly, she took six photographs. Each time, the camera made a soft noise. To Kelly it sounded very loud, but none of the men looked up.

After a minute, she carefully put the camera back in its silver case. Then she looked across at Adam and smiled. She couldn't believe it. 'We've done it!' she thought. 'We've done it!'

Slowly, they both stood up and moved towards the window. Then, suddenly, the floor made a loud noise under Kelly's foot.

'What was that?' said a voice in the room below.

Silence, followed by a second, deeper voice. 'Terry, Dave. Go upstairs and have a look.'

Chapter 7   Escape!

'Let's get out of here!' said Adam. They could hear footsteps coming closer and closer.

Kelly climbed out of the window first. Then Adam quickly passed her the camera case and followed. When he got to the fire-escape, Kelly took his arm. 'Don't move,' she said, 'or they'll hear us.'

A second later, there was a loud crash inside the room. After a few seconds, a voice said, 'There's nothing in here. Let's try next door.'

'Wait!' another voice said. 'I've found something. Look – it's a piece of paper. "Tall Man arrives on Kala–".' The voice suddenly stopped.

Outside on the fire-escape, Kelly closed her eyes. 'Somebody was in here,' the voice said angrily. 'Quick, Terry – the window! I'll go and tell Strang.'

Kelly and Adam turned and ran. Halfway down the fire-escape, they heard somebody above them shout 'Stop!' Then there was the sound of a shot. Kelly looked over her shoulder. A fat man with a beard was standing on the fire-escape. He had a gun in his hand. She turned and ran down the rest of the steps. Adam was waiting for her at the bottom. 'Hurry!' he said. 'We've got to get to the bike.'

The cousins ran as fast as they could along the empty white street. Behind them, they could hear more shots.

'Faster!' Kelly shouted to Adam. Then they were nearly at the corner of Mill Way. Kelly heard the sound of another shot as she reached the motorbike. She looked back. Adam was lying in the snow. His face was white and he was trying to pull himself towards the motor bike. She ran back to him.

'It's my leg,' he said, and pointed to his knee. Blood was running down his jeans.

Kelly knew they didn't have much time. She put Adam's arm around her shoulder and they moved towards the motorbike. He pulled the key out of his pocket.

'You'll have to drive,' he said.

'But I . . .'

'Kelly, I can't drive like this. You'll have to.' They heard the sound of voices shouting in Mill Way. Someone started a car. 'Just do it!' said Adam and pushed the key into Kelly's hand. She took it and helped Adam onto the motorbike. Then she climbed on and turned the key. Nothing happened. 'Go! Go! Go!' Adam shouted.

'I can't start it!' said Kelly. She turned the key again. Still nothing. But the third time it started and, in a cloud of snow, Adam and Kelly drove away.

Above the noise of the motorbike, Adam shouted, 'Let's try to lose them. Quick. Turn left here.'

'OK,' Kelly replied. But it was hard to drive fast in the snow. The motorbike felt like a wild horse under her. Kelly almost crashed it as she turned the first corner.

'Careful!' Adam shouted. After only three or four seconds, they could hear the car behind them again. There were more shots.

Kelly drove faster and faster through the white, empty streets. Then, braking hard, she turned into a narrow road on the right.

'They're getting closer,' Adam shouted. Kelly looked behind her. Adam was right. Then she looked again. A second car was behind them. It had a blue light on the roof.

'Adam! Look!' she shouted. 'It's the police! We're going to be OK. They can't catch us now.' Kelly turned, smiling. Then, suddenly, the smile left her face. In front of them was a canal. She heard Adam's voice in her ear, 'Stop! Stop!', but there wasn't time.

Chapter 8   The Photo of the Year

That evening, George and Rosa went to visit Max in hospital. 'Hi! How do you feel?' Rosa asked, as they walked into the room.

'Not great,' Max said, trying to smile. 'Thanks for coming. Are Kelly and Adam with you?'

George looked at Rosa. A nurse came into the room with two chairs. George thanked her, and he and Rosa sat down.

'What is it?' Max asked. 'Is something wrong? Where are they?'

George looked down at his hands. 'We don't know,' he said. 'Kelly didn't arrive for work this morning. I phoned your house, but there was no answer – not even the answering-machine. Then, a few hours ago, she phoned us. First, she told us about your accident last night. Then she said, "I'm with Adam at a police station in Limehouse."'

'A police station!' Max repeated. 'In Limehouse!'

'That's right,' Rosa said. 'So I asked her why, and she said, "I have to go now. A police car is waiting to take us to Harwich. Tell Uncle Max we'll see him later." Then she put the phone down.'

'Oh, no, they haven't tried to . . .' Max began. But before he could finish the sentence, there was a quiet knock at the door. Rosa got up and answered it. There, looking very tired and cold, were Adam and Kelly.

'Hello, Uncle Max,' Kelly said, trying to smile. She had some flowers in her hand. 'These are for you. I'll go and get some water for them . . .'

'Kelly! Sit down!' said Max. 'You're not going anywhere. I want you and Adam to tell me exactly what's happened.'

Kelly sat on the end of her uncle's bed.

'I'll go and get some more chairs,' George said. 'Why don't you sit here, Adam?'

'Thanks, George,' Adam said. Slowly he walked across the room, holding his right leg.

'And what's the matter with your leg?' Max asked.

'Someone shot me,' Adam replied quietly.

'*Shot* you!!' Rosa said.

'Yes,' Adam answered. 'But I'm OK. Really. It's just a bad cut.'

'I don't believe what I'm hearing,' Max said.

Kelly looked at her cousin. 'Do you want to begin the story?'

Adam told his father about the message on the answering machine, and about their first visit to the hospital.

'Did I say that?' Max asked. 'I don't remember anything.'

Then Adam described what happened at Highgate police station. He explained how Kelly found the note. He told him about the brakes on the car. As the story continued, Max's eyes became wider and wider. 'And you went to Harwich?' he asked.

'Yes,' said Adam. He told his father about the ship and the container, about the journey back to London and then what happened at the warehouse.

'So you got some photos!' Max said.

'Well, yes and no,' Adam replied. 'I'll finish the story.' He described how he and Kelly got out of the warehouse. Then he told his father how their adventure finally ended in an icy canal.

Rosa, sitting next to Adam, had a hand over her mouth. 'But you don't know how to ride a motorbike!' she said to Kelly.

'That's right,' Kelly answered. 'I never tried before today. In Scotland I was too young. But I've watched other people. It wasn't too hard.'

'You mean that was the first . . .' Adam began quietly. His face was going white again.

'But the photos – what about the photos?' Max asked. 'Have you got them?'

Kelly closed her eyes for a minute, then opened them again and looked sadly at her uncle. 'They're at the bottom of the canal. I'm sorry.'

'Oh, no,' Max said and turned his face to the wall for a second.

Then he turned back. 'Poor Kelly,' he said. 'You tried so hard. Tell me what happened next.'

'Well,' Kelly said, 'it was very simple, really. First, the police caught the men in the car. Then they helped Adam and me out of the canal.'

'Did you go back to the warehouse?' George asked.

'Not immediately,' Kelly continued. 'We needed to wait a few minutes for another police car. The police in the first car didn't know anything about the December meeting. They were driving around Limehouse when they heard Strang and the others shooting at Adam and me. They followed the criminals' car and . . .' She lifted both hands in the air.

'OK, so you went back to the warehouse,' said Max.

'Yes,' Kelly continued. 'But by then it was empty. We only found a silver card with the letters *TM* on it.'

'After that, the police drove us to their station in Limehouse and we phoned you,' Adam said to George. 'But we were only there for ten minutes. They gave us some dry clothes, and a doctor looked at my leg. Then we left for Harwich.'

'And did you find the Tall Man? Did you catch him?' Max asked.

'I'm afraid not,' said Kelly sadly. 'The police looked inside every container on the *Kaladis*, but they didn't find anything. He was . . . he was . . . gone.' She could feel tears behind her eyes. 'We were so close, Uncle Max,' she said angrily. 'We had the photos – we had them, and then we–'

Rosa took Kelly's hand. 'It's OK,' she said. 'You did your best.'

After a minute, Kelly stopped crying and turned to her uncle. 'You think we were stupid. You think it was too dangerous.'

'Yes,' Max said. Then he added with a smile, 'But I also think you were both very brave.'

Kelly smiled. 'Thanks.' She wanted to cry again. 'I'm sorry about the photos.'

'You win some and you lose some,' Max said.

Kelly looked at her uncle. Suddenly, she remembered Dr Harris's words on the train three months before: 'Some people are winners and some are losers. You're a winner.'

'Oh, well,' she thought, 'he was nearly right.'

Nobody spoke for a minute. Then Adam slowly stood up, holding his leg. 'Well, Kelly and I must go,' he said. 'The police want to ask us some more questions.'

Suddenly, the door opened and two people walked in. One was Dr Harris and the other was a policeman.

'Hello, Inspector Lane,' said Kelly. She looked at her watch. 'I'm sorry. I know Adam and I are late, but . . .'

The Inspector held up both hands. 'No, no, Miss Logan – that's all right. I wanted to tell you that we've found your camera case at the bottom of the canal.'

'And the film?' Max asked quietly. 'Is it . . . ?'

Inspector Lane smiled. 'There was no water inside the camera.' He turned to Kelly. 'So your photos of the Tall Man are safe.'

Kelly couldn't believe it. 'That's wonderful!' she said. 'When can we see them?'

'Ahhh,' the Inspector said, looking at his hands. 'I'm afraid you'll have to wait for that.'

'What?' Adam said.

'Your photos are very important and we'll need to keep them. Nobody can look at them yet – that means the newspapers, too, of course.'

'But why not?' Rosa asked. 'They're Kelly's photos. She took them!'

'Because the Tall Man mustn't know about them,' said Inspector Lane. He looked at Kelly. 'I'm sorry – I know how important they are to you. But we'll make good use of them. Perhaps after we catch the Tall Man . . .'

Kelly smiled sadly. 'You win some and you lose some,' she repeated softly.

Again, nobody spoke for a minute. Then Inspector Lane turned away. At the door, he stopped.

'I'll be outside when you and your cousin are ready, Miss Logan,' he said. Kelly smiled, and the door closed.

'We must go, too,' George said, standing up. 'But before we do . . .' He turned to Rosa. 'Do you want to tell her?'

'No,' Rosa replied. 'You do it.'

'Well,' George said, 'Jan phoned us this morning.'

'The girl who works for you at the garage?' Kelly asked.

'That's right.'

'Has she had her baby?'

'Last week,' said George. 'And she doesn't want to come back to work. She, her husband and the baby are going to move to Australia.'

'Oh,' said Kelly quietly.

'So we'll need someone new at the garage. A real mechanic.'

'Of course,' Kelly replied, looking at the floor. 'I understand completely. When do you want me to leave?'

George laughed. 'Leave! We don't want you to leave – we want you to *stay*. We want you to be our new mechanic. The job's yours.'

Kelly looked at him, then at Rosa.

Rosa smiled. 'What do you say?'

'I say yes,' Kelly answered. She began to laugh. Then she looked around the room. Adam and Max were laughing, too. 'Oh yes. Yes, *please*!'

ACTIVITIES

Chapters 1–3

Before you read

1 Look at the pictures in *Photo of the Tall Man*. What kind of story do you think it is? Where do you think it happens? Do you think it ends happily or sadly?

2 Find these words in your dictionary. They are all in the story. Use each pair of words in a sentence.

  a *advertisement, mechanic*

  b *crash helmet, motorbike*

  c *expert, jazz*

  d *interview, manager*

3 Answer these questions. Find the words in *italics* in your dictionary.

  a Are you good at *exams*? Why (not)?

  b Can you find the *Isle* of Skye on a map of Britain? Is it part of England, Wales, Scotland or Northern Ireland?

  c Find the story of a *robbery* in today's newspaper. What was taken? How?

After you read

4 Read these five sentences about Kelly's first evening in London. Two of the sentences are true. Which are the true ones?

  a She arrives at King's Cross station.

  b Max meets her at the station.

  c She goes to a party with Adam.

  d She takes a telephone message for Max.

  e She finds a photo of the Tall Man in her uncle's office.

Chapters 4–5

Before you read

5 What do you think is going to happen? Look at:

  a the pictures in these two chapters.

  b the title of each chapter.

6 Find these words in your dictionary. Which can you wear?
brake   dungarees

After you read

7 Discuss why Kelly gets the job at the R and G Garage.

8 Put these sentences from chapters 4 and 5 in the correct order.

    a 'We've got to go to Harwich – now!'

    b 'Will you wait outside for five minutes, Kelly?'

    c 'A man's body was found in the River Thames yesterday evening.'

    d 'He's broken both legs and his right arm.'

    e The next two months were the busiest of Kelly's life.

Chapters 6–8

Before you read

9 Describe the picture on page 29. Start like this: *Adam and Kelly are looking through an opening in the floor. Kelly is holding . . .*

10 Find these words in your dictionary.

    canal   container   dock   ferry   fire-escape
    Inspector   warehouse

    Which one means:

    a a large metal box?

    b a kind of ship?

    c a large building?

    d a man-made river?

    e a place in a port where ships stop?

    f a police officer?

    g steps down the outside of a building?

After you read

11 Answer these questions.

    a At which port does the *Kaladis* arrive?

    b Why is the number 18642 important?

    c Kelly has seen one of the men in the warehouse before. Where? What is his name?

d Why does Kelly have to drive Adam's motorbike after they escape from the warehouse?

e What happens to her photos of the Tall Man?

Writing

12 How did the Tall Man travel to the December meeting? Describe his journey.

13 Imagine you are Kelly or Adam. Write a letter to your grandfather on the Isle of Skye. Tell him about your adventures with the Tall Man.

14 Two weeks after the December meeting, the police catch the Tall Man during a robbery in your country. You are a reporter for an English language newspaper. Write the next day's front page story.

15 It is five years after the end of the story. What has happened in Kelly and Adam's lives? Where do they live? What jobs do they have? Write about the two cousins.